Enid Blyton's

POCKET LIBRARY

PERONEL'S MAGIC POLISH

Illustrated by Sara Silcock

·PARRAGON·

Once upon a time there was a little fairy called Peronel. He lived in the King of Fairyland's palace, and his work was to clean all the brass that the Head Footman brought into the kitchen.

He was very good at this. He would sit all morning, and rub and polish away till the brass fire-irons and trays shone beautifully.

"That's very nice, Peronel," the cook would say to him every morning.

This made him very happy, and he beamed with pride. He thought that no one had ever polished brass as beautifully as he did.

One day, as Peronel sat polishing a brass coal bucket, he had a great idea.

"I know what I'll do!" he said. "I'll invent a new polish that will make everything twice as dazzling as before! I think I know just where to find the right ingredients. How delighted everyone will be!"

So that night he slipped out into the woods and gathered roots and leaves, and a magic flower that only blossomed at midnight, and two cobwebs just newly made. Then he went back to bed.

Next day he boiled everything together, strained it through the cook's sieve, and left it to cool. Then he went to the Wizened Witch, and asked her to sell him a little pot with a brightness spell inside. She told him:

"Empty this into your mixture at sunset, stir it well and sing these words:

'Now the magic has begun,
Polish brighter than the sun!'

Then everything you polish will be brighter than it ever was before!"

"Oh, thank you!" cried Peronel, and ran happily off clutching the little pot, after paying the Wizened Witch a bright new penny he had polished the day before.

When the sun sank slowly down in the sky, Peronel fetched his jar of polish. He emptied the Witch's Spell of Brightness into it, stirred it, and sang:

"Now the magic has begun,
Polish brighter than the sun!"

Next morning Peronel proudly put the polish he had made on the kitchen table, and started work. He had six brass candlesticks to clean and a table lamp. He worked very hard indeed for a whole hour until the cook came into the kitchen. She stopped and threw up her hands in great surprise.

"My goodness, Peronel!" she cried in astonishment. "What *have* you been doing to those candlesticks!

I can hardly look at them, they're so bright!"

"I'm using a magic polish, you see," said Peronel proudly. "Isn't it lovely! I made it all myself!"

The cook called the footmen and the ladies' maids and the butler, to see what a wonderful job Peronel had done.

"Look how bright Peronel has made the candlesticks!" she said. "Isn't he clever? He's made up a magic polish of his own!"

Everybody thought Peronel was certainly very clever indeed, and the little fairy was delighted. But he longed to do something that would make the King and Queen notice him too.

You'd never guess what he did! He fetched the King's golden crown in the middle of the night, and gave it a tremendous polishing with his magic polish! Then he quietly put it back again.

In the morning the King couldn't make out what had happened to his gleaming crown.

"It's so bright I can't bear to look at it," he said to the Queen. "It shines like the sun!"

"Put it on, then your eyes won't be dazzled," said the Queen, and the King took her advice.

But Peronel's polishing had not only made the crown bright, it had made it terribly slippery too, and it

wouldn't stay straight. It kept slipping, first over one ear, then over the other, and everybody in court began to giggle.

The King became quite cross.

"Well, I don't know who's been polishing my crown," he said, "but, anyway, I wish they wouldn't! It's a silly idea!"

Peronel was just nearby, and heard what the King said. Instead of being a sensible little fairy, and deciding not to try to make people praise him any more, he became quite angry.

"All right," he thought. "I'll polish something else tonight! Nobody will know who's done it, and I'll have a bit of fun!"

So the naughty little fairy took his polish and his cloth into the

King's breakfast room that night, and began polishing the gold chairs with all his might.

You can imagine what happened next morning! The King and Queen, the Princess and the Prince, all sat down to breakfast, but they couldn't sit still! They slid and slipped and slithered about on their chairs till the footmen standing behind nearly burst themselves with trying not to laugh!

When the King disappeared under the table, everybody thought it was very funny, even the Queen.

"Dear, dear, dear!" she laughed. "I never saw you disappear so quickly before! I really think we'd better sit on some other chairs until the polish has worn off! Goodness knows who has made them so shining and slippery!"

"I'll soon find out!" said the King crossly, looking very red in the face as he sat down on another chair.

"No, no, dear," said the Queen.
"It was only an accident! Somebody's
been doing his work too well!"

When Peronel heard what had
happened, he was very pleased, and
chuckled loudly. He wished he had
seen it all.

"I'd like to polish something and
see what happens *myself*," he
thought. "Now, what can I polish?
I know! There's a dance tomorrow
night in the ballroom. I'll ask if I

can help to polish the floor, and then I'll hide behind a curtain and see all the people slipping about!"

The naughty little fairy found it was quite easy to get permission to help. The other servants were only too glad to have him, for they all knew how quick and clever he was.

Whilst they were at dinner, he mixed a little of his magic polish into all their pots, and then ran in to his own dinner.

All afternoon Peronel and the other servants polished the floor in preparation for the dance, until it shone like sunlight.

"Dear me!" said the butler, peeping in. "You *have* all worked well!"

He came into the big room – and suddenly his legs slid from beneath him, and he sat down on the floor with a bump.

"Good gracious!" he cried. "Isn't the floor slippery!"

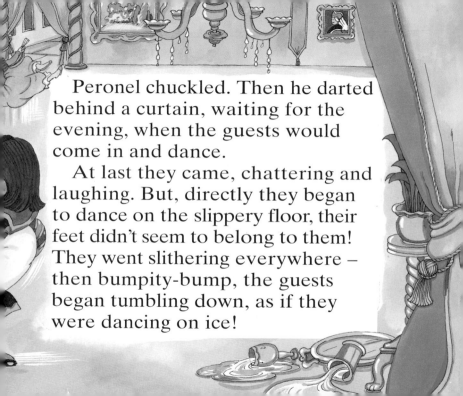

Peronel chuckled. Then he darted behind a curtain, waiting for the evening, when the guests would come in and dance.

At last they came, chattering and laughing. But, directly they began to dance on the slippery floor, their feet didn't seem to belong to them! They went slithering everywhere – then bumpity-bump, the guests began tumbling down, as if they were dancing on ice!

Just then the King came into the ballroom, and stared in the greatest astonishment to see half the dancers on the floor! "What is the matter?" he cried, striding forward.

He soon knew – for his feet flew from under him, and bump! He sat down suddenly.

"Who has polished the floor like this?" he thundered. "It's as slippery as ice. Fetch the servants. I shall punish them!"

Peronel trembled behind the curtain, and wondered what he should do. He wasn't a coward, and he knew he couldn't let the servants be punished for something that was his fault.

So, to the King's surprise, Peronel rushed out from behind the curtain, and ran up to where His Majesty still sat on the floor. But he forgot that it was slippery, and he suddenly slipped, turned head-over-heels, and landed right in the King's lap!

"Bless my buttons!" roared the King in fright. "Whatever's happened now!"

Very frightened indeed, Peronel got up off the King's lap and stood trembling as he confessed what he had done.

"It wasn't the other servants' fault; it was mine," he said. "And it was I who polished your crown the other day, but I only meant to be useful, truly I did!"

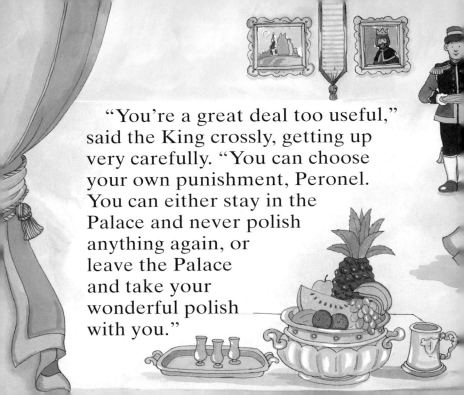

"You're a great deal too useful," said the King crossly, getting up very carefully. "You can choose your own punishment, Peronel. You can either stay in the Palace and never polish anything again, or leave the Palace and take your wonderful polish with you."

Sadly Peronel wondered what to do. "I don't want to do anything else but polish," he said at last. "So I'm afraid I'll have to leave the Palace and take my magic polish with me."

And he did, and what do you suppose he does with it now?

He goes to the fields and meadows and polishes every single golden yellow buttercup that he finds. Look inside one, and you'll see how beautifully he does it!

He misses his friends at the Palace, but now he has made new friends with all the little creatures of the countryside, and he spends his days happily polishing to his heart's content!